OTHER PEOPLE'S PARTIES

A CRACKED SINK STORY

HARAMBEE K. GREY-SUN

HYPERVERSE BOOKS, LLC

Cover design by Kelvin Reese

Cover art copyright © Rolffimages ǀ Depositphotos.com

Published by HyperVerse Books, LLC

www.hyperversebooks.com

Crossing genres without apologies.

Print ISBN-13: 978-1-64044-013-5

OTHER PEOPLE'S PARTIES

MY INVITATION to an office holiday party had come courtesy of a brick.

Actually a packaged fruitcake that was shaped like a brick and pretty much felt like a brick against my shoulder when Sharene's latest beau tossed it through the window of my Camaro SS at the intersection of Edson and Clarke.

One could curse the dreary yet mild December day that had inspired me to drive home with my windows down in the first place—but I'd preferred to curse the other drivers and the rain-drizzle-slicked roads as I tried tailing Derrick Trainor's silver Beemer without acquiring yet another dent.

I might've washed out of the police academy, but there were certain skills I'd honed long before I ever even dreamed about becoming a cop. Maneuvering muscle monsters on crowded and otherwise treacherous downtown city streets while fleeing actual cops had been one of them. As was getting a good look of someone at just a glance.

Neither Derrick nor Sharene had likely imagined I'd recognize either of them in their speeding BMW i8, let alone follow them or even make my way into the lobby of the museum. And yet, here we were: Me in a standoff with a defensive line of security guards and Derrick right behind them, standing on the raised edge of the huge decorative water fountain and giving me the finger. Sharene stood farther back in the distance with the other partygoers, looking on.

The air was thick with the scent of pine, the clinking of champagne glasses, and the well-dressed crowd's murmuring—much of it probably about me. Apparently the museum was hosting a private holiday event for the employees of the financial tech company SimSan, a fact I only realized after I just missed getting my hands on Derrick.

It seemed like I was always breaking up other people's parties.

"Get out of my way!" I shouted for the third or fourth time. "I'm with the police department!"

"Then where's your badge?" came the refrain from one of the guards.

"This guy!" Derrick shouted. "Pretending to be a cop!"

Yeah—it was a hot button alright, and some people really knew how to push it. Even women I only dated for a couple of weeks. I had known Sharene's new beau by sight. I hadn't known he worked for one of the hottest young companies in Synchrony. Nor did I know he had probably been dialing nine-one-one while I had been chasing him.

Actual sworn officers, some in uniform, were soon on the scene with me—in front of me—taking the place of the security guards in shielding me from everyone else. Standing tall among them all was Sergeant Roxana Spiegel, her lips curling as she squared up with me.

"Too much rum cake, Moreno?"

I opened my mouth, swallowed what I was about to say, then tried again. "I was assaulted—"

"Crap like this," she snarled, "is exactly why you never would've made it as a police officer. You should feel lucky enough we even allow you on the department premises. You better believe I'll be talking to someone about that little perk. For now, I don't want to see you again until the new year. Maybe not even then."

"But—"

"Get out of my sight or get arrested."

I got to my car, shaking my head at the state of the city and its police department.

There were dedicated cops; there were superstar cops; there were *legits*—men and women who were average performers but on the up-and-up. Still, too many who wore the badge thought that shield might be replaced with actual gold if they just played their cards right. "To protect and to serve . . ." the moneyed interests. The more money a citizen of Synchrony had, the more interested many cops became in actually doing their sworn duty.

Kiss my foul blessings that I'd avoided being inducted into the blue fraternity—I guess.

A cocktail of bad temper, overeager ambition, and a little too much of the "pastimes with brandy and wine" had gotten me booted from the academy. After a dark stint of mastering the arts of hacking, I eventually cleaned myself up enough to alter my career and still find my way into law enforcement—just in a much different city from where I'd started. Anuba, my wife at the time, hadn't stayed long enough to see me get sober, let alone cheer me on as I got a job as a civilian crime scene technician. Maybe it was just as well. My ambition and temper had remained with me.

And maybe—just maybe—that's what drew the bad-luck women to me. Professional ladies with class and stylish drapings that hid ill-mannered chassis. I often found out rather quickly that such women preferred bad-boy drivers. That wasn't me.

My flare-ups were consistently directed at men. And once that nasty fact was discovered, the "professional lady" I happened to be dating—Sharene being the latest and worst—would want little more to do with me. But having a short-and-sweet breakup was not in their nature. Sharene and the other lovers of "true" bad boys each dragged me through a long goodbye, which involved them abusing my property, dating other men, and goading such men into further abusing my property while taunting me—with words, or mud-caked shoes, or fruitcakes. Sometimes the taunts worked too well.

After the cranking elevator deposited me onto the familiar floor of my apartment building, I trudged down the hall toward my door at the farthest end of the 7-shaped hallway, taking in the Christmas cheer of roasting meats and vibrant herbs, a reminder of long-past holidays spent with Anuba, when she used to make lemon-rosemary roasted turkey.

As I rounded the sharp curve, however, traces of a harsh scent intruded. With each step, the repugnant smell developed a picture in my mind: charred flesh.

I slowed my pace yet darted my eyes left and right, eventually fixing them on the doorway up ahead on my right, the entrance to unit 106. The apartment door was ajar.

Cautiously I approached until I was standing at the threshold, attempting to peer through the crack. The foyer was dark, but lights were on somewhere deeper in the apartment. I heard the faint notes of music. Adult contemporary. Familiar old standards, yet refreshingly non-holiday related. The aroma of honey-glazed carrots and traces of cabbage reached me—but the burnt scent of meat scrunched my nose and made me more careful about inhaling deeply.

"Hello? Anyone here?" I held my breath for a few moments, straining to pick up a response or the sounds of movement. I only heard the faint yet dulcet voice of Johnny Mathis flowing from whatever speakers.

With the tip of my loafer, I nudged the door open further and stepped inside. I ventured a "Hello" again but had already given up on hearing the same from someone else's lips.

Using my shoe to gently close the door behind me, I kept my hands close, ready for any defensive measures that might be called for, hoping that hands would be enough.

I entered a Spartan living area holding just the basics of comfort, no artwork or decorations other than the artificial Christmas tree over by the cracked-open window in the corner. From what I could make out in the somber room, the plastic tree was stingy with ornaments and draped in a string of lights that were either turned off or not working. The furnishings were nothing to look at twice. Aside from the sofa, there was little for anyone to hide behind. The room was dead.

I made my way toward the music and glowing light —the kitchen. As I neared the doorless entrance, I saw a white, laceless sneaker lying on its side, a few inches away from the bare foot it had once cradled.

I hesitated, stilled my breathing. I wasn't scared of a

dead body—I'd seen more than my fair share—but I was listening for the beating heart or faint exhalations of a possible murderer lurking nearby. Hearing nothing, I edged into the small U-shaped nook of a kitchen, my eyes furtively searching about while taking in glimpses of the body on the stained linoleum.

Sprawled stomach-down, the woman wore a gray sweatshirt, faded jeans, and one white, laceless tennis shoe on her left foot. She'd tawny skin, long dark hair. An overturned bar stool lay across her back. A fork and other objects were scattered about on the floor, as were the dark stains—liquids that had not yet fully dried.

None of the spilled substances appeared to be blood. But I had no idea what spilled liquids might be under her.

The women's head was turned to the left—eyes closed, mouth open.

I gingerly stepped closer, trying not to disturb anything as I attempted to get near enough to determine if she was still breathing. All the while, I kept my ears perked for any sounds in the apartment not made by me or Manilow, whose voice now crooned from the portable radio on the countertop.

She was still breathing. There was a small cut on the forehead; what little blood was there had dried. I positioned her on her back, loosened her clothing, and checked her airway. I then glanced about, assessing the scene and checking for lingering dangers while also searching for something to elevate her feet.

Neither the oven nor the cooktop was on. Food had been prepared. Some of it was in proper dishes; some of it was spilled; all of it was scattered about the stove's adjacent counters, messy in the way that no multi-tasking cook could avoid when readying a meal. Here, it seemed a lot of effort had gone into preparing a meal for one.

A prepared plate of honey-glazed carrots, roasted cabbage with walnut bits, and caramelized mashed potatoes rested on a placemat next to the radio. Cold, yet still wickedly aromatic up close. Two small dishes of dried fruits were nearby. Four roasted duck breasts sat in a pan on the stove. It appeared they'd had a rough time of it in the oven. The woman had likely been on the verge of settling in for her lonely meal at the kitchen counter when she was attacked.

She'd keep breathing, but she wasn't coming to. I pushed a familiar pattern of buttons of my phone and shouted the emergency to the woman who answered.

My cell phone remained tight in my right hand as I checked the rest of the house, already reasonably confident whoever else had been here had long fled.

Suspicion confirmed, I returned to the kitchen to treat the cut and do whatever else I could for the poor woman while I waited. Rather than calling dispatch, I had dialed Roxana's direct number. I'd a feeling my word-barrage would provoke more immediate results.

———

I withstood Roxana's usual dressing-down and ignored most of it, listening only to any questions or comments she barked my way that pertained to the matter at hand. I pushed most of my attention to the responders who saw to the woman and commented on her injuries.

When prompted, I told Roxana what I knew then nodded with deaf ears to the insults and threats. Once she ran out of breath, I promised to give whatever statement needed to be given at the station later.

Back in my own apartment, I sat in my recliner, in the dark. My thoughts couldn't leave the unconscious woman. She lived three doors down from me and I didn't even know her name. I'd seen her in passing, but we'd never spoken. I recalled she never wore makeup, never smiled, fleetingly made eye contact, and never said a word to anyone—at least not that I'd ever heard. I'd always considered her plainly pretty, church-mouse quiet, and evidently hurting—emotionally, at the very least. And now ...

I turned on the nearest lamp, picked up my phone. I still had some genuine friends in the Synchrony PD and even a few more who owed me a favor or two.

Luckily I didn't need to call in a favor to find out her

name—Ria Santos Guardiola—and which hospital they'd taken her to.

On the drive over I had a momentary worry about bypassing security, but I soon learned the hospital staff were dealing with their own version of seasonal spirits.

The place was a madhouse with men and women in scrubs, security uniforms, and—yes—even a few police uniforms running to and fro, attempting to handle a variety of tantrums, scuffles, and other emergencies. All it took to get Ms. Guardiola's room number from a harried nurse was me shouting the woman's name and that I was with the police. Granted, with the constant telephone ringing and the intercom blaring nonstop, it took several attempts on my part—but I got it.

Weaving my way through the pandemonium, I was bumped and jostled more than once as the alternating scents of pine cleaner, vomit, bleach, and blood pummeled my olfactory system. Once I had the closed door in sight, I found an out-of-the-way-spot to lurk. I watched the beige wooden door for a good fifteen minutes or so, waiting to see if doctors or nurses—or actual men or women with badges—passed in or out. For all the activity I saw, the room may as well have been empty.

I momentarily cheered myself with the idea that, long before I'd arrived, the doctors and nurses had swooped in, doing all the procedures the woman's insurance permitted them to; meanwhile some actual badges had been around to question her and would type up a detailed report later.

Yeah. Fat chance on all of that happening.

I knocked on the door, possibly heard a muffled response, then turned the knob.

"Hello—?" I began in only to be taken aback by the almost overwhelming scent of something bitter. The hissing hand sanitizer dispenser hanging to my left, next to the door, seemed to be malfunctioning.

I gently closed the door behind me and stepped forward, hoping there might be flowers or a fresh fruit bowl somewhere deeper in the room.

Ms. Guardiola lay in a reclining position, her wavy dark brown hair cascading over her shoulders and clashing with the gaudy hospital gown. My footsteps on the wooden floor turned her head slightly toward me. Through heavy lids, she watched as I padded to the foot of her bed so she could see me without straining. I watched her in turn, trying to determine if she'd any bruises I'd missed in her apartment.

Other than a bandage on her forehead, her smooth skin seemed undamaged. I smiled at that. In response, the corners of her lips turned downward.

What a way to make my official introduction to a neighbor.

"Ms. Guardiola? My name is Ruben Moreno."

Her lips parted slightly as she studied my face. I was ninety-one percent certain she identified the name as Filipino and, rather than ask and possibly offend, she was trying to find a match with my features. I just tried to get her off the subject.

"I'm with the Synchrony PD."

Her parted lips released a sigh. ". . . Yeah." Her voice was a little hoarse. "The doctor told me I'd been found in my apartment, unconscious. I was wondering if the police were going to show up, tell me what happened."

"I'd rather you tell me what happened."

She attempted a shrug. "How would I know? One moment I was cooking—trying to, anyway—then the next minute, I'm waking up here."

"You live alone?"

She nodded.

"Did you have anyone over this evening? Does anyone have a key?"

She shook her head to both.

"Well then do you normally leave your door unlocked?"

Anger unsettled her placid expression. "*Why* would I —" A sudden realization seemed to sap what little energy indignation had given her. ". . . *damn*. The *smoke*."

"Smoke?"

"I was cooking duck in the oven. And I guess it wasn't as clean as it was supposed to be."

"The duck?"

"The *oven*. A couple of the detectors went off. I was scrambling around, fanning the smoke away from the alarms, turning on fans and opening windows. I must've opened my front door too. Maybe with all the running around, I tripped and hit my head. Or—" She winced as she tried to lean forward from her pillow and reconsidered. "Do you . . . You think someone might've come in?"

I didn't know what to think at this point. "May I ask what you do for a living?"

"Why?"

"It might give a clue as to who attacked you—assuming someone did." Might—but it wasn't the primary reason I wanted to know.

"I own a couple of flower shops. So what?"

So the police likely wouldn't do an investigation, even if she asked for one. She wasn't important enough —lacked the silver, green, or gold sheen that widened authorities' eyes and made them swoon. She had no one. Except me.

She raised her left hand to her bandage, patted it. "You think someone out there received a flower arrangement that set them off? They mistook it for an edible and tried to eat the daisies?"

I couldn't tell if she was being snarky or serious—but it did spark another question. "Why did you say 'trying to' cook, earlier? Is that not a usual thing for you?"

"I cook all the time. But . . ."

I narrowed my eyes. "What?"

"Nothing . . ." Her eyes closed.

"Ms. Guardiola"—I raised my voice, hoping to get her to focus—"I think this could be helpful."

"Was just going to say that sometimes I like to try new flavors."

She spoke drowsily. *Fine.* I doubt I'd get very far with an interrogation anyway, especially considering I'd never been trained in the skill. It would only be a matter of time before she started asking me questions.

I thanked her for her time and bid her good night—though I'm not sure she heard it.

———

I called in one of my favors with an occasional buddy of mine at the PD. In turn, he contacted the hospital in a more official capacity than I had. Later, he called me back to give me the rundown. Ms. Guardiola had no fresh bruises other than the one on her head, likely sustained from her fall. I paired that with the fact that there'd been no signs of forced entry.

So what had caused her to fall? Was she not able to ventilate the place sufficiently, so the smoke got to her?

Or did someone slip in after she started opening doors and windows?

The PD couldn't have cared less. My buddy told me she'd already been written off as home-accident case. No crime. I'd wager she was already pretty much forgotten once Roxana and her crew left the apartment building. With the holidays, all badges in this city had only two concerns. Spending time with their families, keeping them safe and embraced, and maintaining a lookout for more serious crimes, ensuring they didn't blossom. Couldn't blame them. But I couldn't just turn my back on Ms. Guardiola.

Since it just happened to be on the way home, I decided to return to the scene.

The badges hadn't even taped it off. No crime scene to them. They were, however, courteous enough to lock the door, which—after retrieving the necessary tools and gloves from my apartment—I easily picked.

The badges hadn't tidied up the place. In fact, judging by the state of the kitchen, it seemed they'd done nothing but close the door behind them after the body had been removed. I was grateful.

I turned off the portable radio—having a care for the woman's utility bills—and focused on those duck morsels. She'd been preparing a meal for one but had prepared four portions—I readily assumed for meals later in the week. But a longer look showed that she had cut a slice from each one. I then figured she was sampling to see which she preferred for her evening meal.

Each breast had been seasoned simply, yet differently—likely so that she could use one pan for all. I bent my nose closer. One smelled predominantly of cinnamon; another of garlic and rosemary, with hints of pepper. The third was lemon-peppery. The fourth was weird. At first I figured Chinese five-spice—but there was something else there.

I checked around, pulling open every drawer, cabinet door, and countertop compartment, finding the shakers and other containers for all the spices I'd identified. The spices that hadn't been used were all in the under-the-counter spice rack—labeled, recognizable, and not out of the ordinary.

Taking note again of the dried, sticky spillage on the linoleum, I crouched down and continued the search on my hands and knees. It was soon clear Ms. Guardiola wasn't one for mopping—not often at least.

I found a few stray rice particles, some old, dried pasta strands, some shriveled wisps of kale, and eventually—wedged slightly between two of the cookbooks arrayed in a wire mesh basket adjacent to the refrigerator—a translucent packet filled with a dirty rainbow of particles. The packet had no label, but I could easily figure the source. As could anyone the least bit familiar with Synchrony's underground.

I cracked open the packet and charily inhaled,

picking up notes of pepper, cinnamon, cloves, star anise, and a few things I couldn't readily pinpoint. What had landed Ms. Guardiola in the hospital was no longer a mystery. From simply inhaling, I felt myself getting woozy and had little trouble imaging what would have happened if I had, say, dabbed my finger in the spice and licked it.

Why would she feel the need for such an exotic spice when every other ingredient was relatively banal? From the looks of things, she hadn't even yet worked her way up to red wine sauce.

I thought hard but not long about removing evidence from the scene. As far I was concerned, I was the lone investigator on an incident only I saw as a crime. I had a right to take it—to guard it.

On my way out, I glanced at the Christmas tree, again wondering why its lights weren't on. Approaching, I saw the cord had been unplugged. Maybe Ms. Guardiola had tripped over it while hustling to open the adjacent window.

She must've jostled the end table as well. A photo frame lay on its back. Inside was a picture of two smiling figures, arms around each other's shoulders. Ria Santos Guardiola and a much younger man—maybe thirteen years old. Likely her son.

She hadn't always been alone.

———

I'd spent more than my fair share of time collecting evidence at scenes where folks had partied a little too hard with mind-altering substances. More often than not, there was an indirect line of evidence from the scene to an Yndikas store.

There were maybe a half dozen in the city, most of them in or near the downtown area. The specialty shops offered a wide variety of spices and teas, though nothing that one could find in a conventional grocery store. Yndikas specialized in the unusual, the quirky, the outré. Even when their peppers or sugars or herbs or whatever seemed—by name and appearance—to be relatively unexceptional, there was always just a twist. Not just imported black peppercorns, but uniquely smoked pepper from some tiny Asian island no one had ever heard of. Not just pink sugar crystals, but sweet magenta crystals sourced from somewhere in South America.

All such items were courtesy of the Chark clan, the professional "family" that controlled Synchrony's exotic spice trade. It was said that some of their signature blends would make driftwood taste like a Kobe beef steak. What many actually knew and often turned a blind eye to was that certain spice blends had the same effect as nicotine, or opioids, or some other among a wide variety of harmful drugs.

Having nothing better to do on yet another drizzling

yet mild December day, I set out for the closest establishment.

The Yndikas store's interior had an almost laughable bucolic look with its walls of rustic brickwork, creaky wooden floors, and seemingly randomly placed wooden barrels displaying wicker baskets stuffed with hand-tied plastic bags of all sorts of edibles. One could easily get lost among the mazes of shelves, which is undoubtedly why the staff made a point to stand out among the patrons by wearing brown bib overalls over blue shirts. While wandering through, handing out the occasional free sample, they helped customers get to where they wanted to be. And there was always a heaping helping of customers.

Some wandered through with glassy eyes. Others zipped through, as if partaking in a scavenger hunt on a treacherous obstacle course. The most serious customers only came after freshly bathed, wearing no make-up or perfumes, and garbed themselves in fragrance-free clothing so that, when considering a purchase via their sense of smell, there'd be less to interfere with their decision-maker.

I'd done my best to fit in with this third grouping. But wandering among the rows of shelves upon shelves of carefully arranged bottles, jars, and hanging ziplocked bags—all of which allowed the seepage of smells, even if just a little—I couldn't figure how one would be able to perfectly isolate a scent no matter how closely the container was held to one's nose. Just walking through the sugars section, my salivary glands began working overtime. I swallowed so much I worried I might have a new type of diabetes by the time I left.

But that was the least of my worries. Passing through a section of essential oils, I got the sense of someone eying me. A glance over my shoulder gave me the image of a tall man, fortyish, with a precision-trimmed goatee. He was dressed in a three-piece suit, a pricey one.

Aware he was following me, I tried to ignore him as I (finally) made my way into the section of spice blends specifically for meats. I eyed each package quickly but carefully, looking for contents that came close to the packet in my coat pocket. After a little more than five minutes of fruitless searching, I heard someone stepping up close behind me.

"Can I help you find something?" asked a deep voice.

I turned to see the man in the suit, standing just a couple of feet from me. When I tilted my chin upward to meet his eyes, he raised his right hand to his left shoulder and dusted off something that certainly wasn't there. The calling card of the Chark. Dusting imaginary "spice" off of their shoulders was a way of telling folks like me who they were while signaling that they were untouchable. I wasn't in the mood to be intimidated.

I removed the packet from my pocket and thrust it toward his nose. "Do you carry this?"

His eyes remained on mine. "No."

"What do you mean? How do you know?"

"It's not in the store packaging," he monotoned.

"So what?" I said. "It's an exotic spice. That's what you guys specialize in, right?"

His eyes narrowed as he looked me up and down. "Maybe you want a different store."

A threat—one that would be plenty scary under the right circumstances. To me, it was just a signal that I was wasting my time in this particular location.

I turned a shoulder to the goon and headed for the exit.

Passing a checkout counter on my way, two items caught my eye. One was a sticker stating that one could pay with cash, credit, or via SimSan. The other was a stack of postcards—invitations to a customer appreciation event taking place in two days.

I snatched a card and pushed out into the cold.

———

I fast-walked the wet, cobblestone sidewalks in a haphazard fashion—looking over both shoulders, trying not to slip or bump into holiday shoppers, and blinking every so often when a random flake got into my eye. The day had gone from decidedly mild to decidedly not, threatening to inject snow flurries into the gray gloom.

Once satisfied I wasn't being followed, I made my way to The Big Roast, a farm-to-cup coffee shop perpetually enveloped in an unseen cloud of burnt chocolate and scorched earth. Only die-hard coffee fans pushed their way through such fragrant smog to pay mucho dollars for the delicacies offered. I was a happened-to-be-in-the-neighborhood fan who presently purchased the cheapest cup and got a choice seat where I could do some peaceful research.

Absent my laptop, I had to use my phone. Thankfully, it was a mighty powerful one.

SimSan was a relative newcomer to the financial tech industry. Successful and known, but not in the top five among companies offering similar services. I wasn't even sure about top ten. For an establishment like Yndikas to trust them . . . What other sorts of outfits trusted them?

Couldn't dig up much using just my phone, but the information I found was intriguing.

I ordered another large cup of coffee to go, this time something more exotic—Ecuador Finca el Chito. Once I got home, I planned to go much deeper into the dirt.

———

At home with bigger and better equipment, I played some hunches, utilized my old hacking skills, and uncovered a longer list of SimSan's clients than the one advertised on their site. An interesting roster of businesses. Some of them, I knew, had ties to organized crime.

Researching further, it wasn't a huge shock to discover that SimSan itself wasn't squeaky clean, not even in dealings with entities a simpleton would think twice about screwing over.

I narrowed on SimSan's relationship with the Chark's legitimate businesses, including the Yndikas stores. Found some juicy tidbits, hints of malfeasance here and there, much of it discussed or alluded to in the company's internal documents and communications. There was enough to make me salivate at all that a proper audit might bring to light.

An intentionally confusing pricing structure for transaction fees. Junk fees for services that shouldn't have any cost associated with them. Retaining a significant percentage of the original processing fee when a business refunds a customer. These and other shenanigans, most of them involving tiny amounts that added up. I'd wager they used similar schemes on multiple clients. Maybe on all of them. Or maybe just the ones that had too many transactions and raked in too much dough to notice, which is what such rip-off companies counted on.

This is what it looked like to me: Those running SimSan were just another gang of wealthy criminals. A fearless or very stupid gang.

If that were truly the case, then maybe a few of their equally shady clients would hold them to account, if enough of them knew about the company's schemes. Or maybe it would take just one shady client.

———

After I completed my research, I called the hospital to check up on Ms. Guardiola's status and found that she'd been released while I was out pounding cobblestones. I freshened my breath and sauntered over to her apartment, enjoying the smells of cinnamon and orange peel that wafted through the hallway while also trying to block out some irritating tune about Santa Claus, beer, and bratwurst.

The bad music was coming from a neighbor, but—stopping in front of Guardiola's door—it was clear the smells were coming from her apartment. Had she already gone back to baking?

I knocked. After a second round, she pulled open the door with a somewhat dazed look. She'd a smaller bandage on her forehead.

"Oh. Officer—"

Shaking my head, I raised my hands palms out. "I'm not an officer."

Her eyebrows knit together as she frowned. "So . . . what were you doing in my hospital room?"

"I *am* with the police department, but—"

"What is *wrong* with this city? All the real cops take a break for the holidays?"

I stifled a joyless chuckle. "You must be new in town."

She glared at me, a prelude—I knew—to her slamming the door in my face. I raised my hands again, pleading.

"I'm not a sworn officer, but I *am* concerned about your accident. I'm trying to get to the root of it. Do you . . . Do you mind if I come in?"

She gave me a hesitant once-over before sighing and stepping backward, pulling the door open wider.

I shuffled in, my eyes involuntarily drifting to the left, sweeping over the end table with its framed photo and a steaming cup of tea, the source of the orange peel and cinnamon aromas. My gaze landed on the twinkling Christmas tree. "*Nice.*"

Ms. Guardiola slid into my field of view. "*Why* are you here?"

I cleared my throat. "I, uh, actually live down the hall from you. We've never met—I mean, not before the hospital—but, well—"

"*Yes?*"

"I was the one who found you unconscious, in the

kitchen." I reached into my coat pocket. "I also found this."

I held the packet up near my face. Her eyes widened at the sight of it, but she said nothing.

"Do you remember where you got it?"

Her eyes shifted to mine, but her lips remained closed.

"It's okay. As I said, I'm not a cop."

"But you're still with the SPD. And some of us know what that really stands for."

Yeah—*Stinkin' Pig Doo*—among other far more profane expansions. I didn't care to hear her preferred version. "I'm a crime scene technician. And I think your accident had something to do with this stuff."

Her eyes flicked from mine to the packet and narrowed, perhaps trying to make the connection. ". . . You think I was poisoned?"

I nodded.

She turned her back to me, gazing (perhaps) at the fake tree with its dozens of winking lights.

"I bought it . . ." Her voice was weary. "I bought it from one of the guys who makes deliveries to my shops."

"A delivery guy?" I repositioned myself between her and the tree. "Why?"

"*Because*," she gnarred, "I'm *friendly* with everyone I do business with. Customers, cleaning staff, *and* delivery men. I strike up conversations. This particular gentleman also happened to be something of a simple-food hobbyist—those who take a minimalist approach to making the relatively ordinary extraordinary. From time to time, I like to try new and unusual spices."

From time to time, she liked to get a little high as well. "You know, they have stores for folks like you."

"I don't shop at the Yndikas stores anymore. I don't like their management. The way they do business . . ."

Neither did I. But by trying to be evasive, she was saying more than she realized.

"One of their acquisition folks have a meeting with you?"

She blinked, slowly. "Yeah—and I have serious questions about their code of ethics. But why do you care? You can't do anything. You're not a cop."

No, I wasn't—but I was close enough that it was often easy to forget that most folks in this unfair city didn't eat from the same pie of common knowledge as those of us adjacent to law enforcement. Most folks knew nothing of the Charks. Even folks who may've had some vague sense that some unsavory folks owned the Yndikas shops, and maybe even had an idea of what was bought and sold in the back rooms, they probably didn't know these same unsavory folks had street runners, back-alley dealers, and door-to-door salespersons—spice-slingers in a variety of uniforms operating a variety of hustles while peddling off-market substances. They'd gotten to Ms. Guardiola, just via another route.

"Where's your son, Ms. Guardiola?" I pointed a pinkie toward the photo, making a big assumption about the boy in it.

"My son? What—? *What* does he have to do with anything?"

"You keep a picture of him and you together, prominent so that you can't but help to see it. But there're no presents under the tree. We're a little over a week away from Christmas, and you like to cook, but based on what's in your refrigerator and freezer, you're not planning on making anything special, and certainly not for more than one person. You have a guest bedroom, but it's in no condition to receive guests. And—"

"You've been through my house?" Her whole body shook as she stared daggers.

I sighed. "I told you, I'm a crime scene tech—"

She thrust a flat-palmed hand toward me like traffic cop trying to stop a vehicle speeding toward a busy crosswalk.

"I *heard* you. And just you forget about my son." She turned a shoulder and shuffled between coffee table and couch, muttering, "He's certainly forgotten about me."

I approached the table nearest the Christmas tree and lifted the framed photo of mother and son, both bearing goofy grins. Slightly blurry cherry blossoms served as an in-picture frame; the Washington monument—engulfed in blue scaffolding—stood in the distant background. Mother and son, touristing, care-free. "When did he run away?"

I pivoted toward her, finding her not sitting on the couch, but still standing, wide-eyed, mouth gaping, arms folded, as if she just couldn't believe my audacity.

After a moment, she lowered her chin, shook her head, sighed. ". . . A few years ago. First week of January. He was a good student; had a great mind for chemistry and biology; and he'd been trying to get into some really good schools. He didn't. Not into any of the ones he wanted. And . . . Well, we always have—*had*—a special meal on New Year's Day. Really elaborate, just the two of us. I screwed up a new recipe, stuffing a bird. He got sick, blamed me. Said I tried to poison him, to get back at him for not doing as well as I expected. As I wanted. As I *demanded*.

"*Yes*, I always pushed him, wanted the best for him —and maybe I should be sorry for that—but I certainly didn't try to poison him!"

I nodded. "He didn't believe you, so he went out into the world to become a success on his own terms."

"I went to the police, but . . . This *rotten* city."

"Since his departure, you've dialed back on the complex recipes, stuck to relatively simple dishes, kicked up with spice."

"What else *can* I do? After what happened, I can't trust myself." Her eyes moistened. "Hell, maybe this time, deep down, I did know that what I bought was really poison. Maybe I wanted to pay myself back for pushing him away. Maybe deep down, in my heart and soul, I believed I deserved death."

The tears began. I glanced around the room for a box of tissue I already knew wasn't there.

"John Mark . . ." Sobbing, she wiped her cheeks with the backs of her wrists. "*He* was my heart and soul. And Heaven knows how he ended up."

Heaven might've known for certain—but I had an idea.

———

The Synchrony PD had something of a détente with the city's wealthier criminal element. So long as they didn't commit any truly heinous crimes—no bloodbaths, no stuff not easily hidden from the general populace—they were free to operate at will, so long as they paid a fair tax. The percentage of tax paid to the city's officials differed depending on how deep the pockets of the syndicate in question.

When it came to funds, the Charks were swimming in it.

For their afternoon customer appreciation event, they'd rented an entire park, downtown near the financial district, and populated it with fiddlers, carolers, bell jinglers, and other entertainers, to say nothing of the abundant purveyors of sweet and tasty tidbits. Despite the morning snowfall experienced by the rest of the city, they'd kept the walkways shoveled and ice-free. They'd planned well, investing in outdoor flame heaters and housing warm beverage stations under spacious red and white winter party tents.

In any other city, such an event would see the presence of a uniformed cop every hundred feet or so, at the very least to provide a sense of safety. Not here—and no one seemed much bothered by the fact. Likely, those who cared about such silly matters as security noticed the men in fine three-piece suits, trench coats, and—some of them—fedoras. These men milled about singly or in pairs under the tents, or they patrolled the walkways, holding large umbrellas aloft to keep the sparse flurries from dampening their threads.

But the SPD weren't fools. Officers were stationed just outside the perimeter of the event, ready to run in if needed. Détente or not, they weren't going to allow public mayhem. Just as they certainly wouldn't allow any member of a known criminal syndicate to remain anonymous. The PD kept photos and files on every known member of the Chark family; and over the past couple of days, I'd put in a lot of late-night overtime—unpaid, of course.

As I weaved through the merry throngs, getting jostled by puffy-coated revelers or nearly tackled by screaming and headlong-running children, I didn't avert my eyes when nearing any of the fine-suited thugs. I glanced at the face of every single one. Most paid me no attention. Why should they? I was just one out of probably a thousand freeloaders who crammed into the park to live it up, perhaps snagging a few sample edibles and spice packets in the bargain. I kept my gloved hands in my coat pockets, despite the scent of roasting chestnuts triggering a hunger for something warm, crisp, and nutty.

After an hour of walking, I was ready to plant my bottom in a chair—then I spotted him. He stood alone not too distant from the ice skating rink. He wore a trench coat and suit like all the others and a fedora like some, but his umbrella was folded under his arm, allowing flurries to fall on his hat and coat.

I crunched through the snow-covered grass as a shortcut. He seemed entranced by the skaters, terrible as they were, falling on their rears as they attempted simple patterns. Perhaps he was more focused on the older folks skating with the younger. Parents enjoying time with their children. He was at least seven years removed from the age of thirteen, but there was no mistaking him.

I spoke when I was within shouting distance. "John Mark . . ."

His face whipped in my direction, his eyes glaring. "*What*? Who are you?"

I gave one answer to both questions. "Hopefully a beacon."

He turned his entire body to face me now, squaring up, his eyes narrowing. Despite the garb, despite his association, he was far from intimidating. Not only was I twice his age and bigger than him, his posture told me his hand-to-hand skills were lacking.

"Get lost," he growled.

"You've got it wrong. You're the lost one. I'm the rescuer."

He stepped forward, reaching for his umbrella. "I told you—"

"Your mother. *Ria.* Some time ago, your associates approached her with a proposition to become business partners. They promised to help her expand her flower shops. A small acquisition. Adding to their roster of legit enterprises. It would've been kind of like a hobby to them at first. But if they managed to get one of their in-development ideas off the ground—exotic flowers that exude mind-altering fragrances—they'd have an avenue for distribution. Your mom likely didn't know about their ideas, but she was still wise enough to turn them down."

John Mark's face was a storm of rage, but he stayed his hand, undoubtedly wondering if I was on the level.

I continued, "You might think it's not wise to turn down such propositions. You're right. But since the Charks have to stay on the right side of the law, they couldn't just handle her directly. Well, they could, but they'd rather not. Luckily, they found you, likely on the streets or grouped in some abandoned dwelling with some other runaway teens. Once they found out about your great mind for chemistry, they offered you a job, tutored you in their way of mixology. I'll wager you were a fast learner. I'd double down that soon you were coming up with your own special blends." I retrieved the packet from my pocket, held it up eye-level. "Recognize it?"

He said nothing, but his expression told the tale.

"I got it from your mother. They sold it to her."

Slowly, he shook his head. "So?"

"So it's poison. They took one of your blends, added an extra element. They came up with a way for you to poison your own mother, getting their revenge. Their version of a sick joke, one you would be left out of. But, even if you happened to find out that it was your blend that had done it, and if you happened to have a problem with it, your business associates could point the finger at you, maintain plausible deniability—*Why would we ever want to deliberately poison anyone? Why wouldn't the bratty son want to? He is an angry, resentful runaway after all.* You'd go to jail—alone. *Or,* you'd get set up in the flower business, take on a new hobby. Shall I go on?"

His lips bared back, revealing teeth that appeared ready to bite through bone. But he took a breath, swallowed, and shook his head.

"Your mom didn't take enough of the poison to kill

her. Eventually she would have, with too much sprinkled on a piece of meat."

He looked past me now, his eyes focused on nothing. "She misses you."

"Well," he mumbled, "she'll see me when she sees me."

"When you make of a success of yourself? Keep hanging around this scum, and you'll be a success all right."

John Mark's eyes widened. The "nothing" behind me had been replaced by "something." Before I could look over my shoulder, I heard the deep voice. "Problem here?"

I turned around, meeting the stern visages of two trenchcoated men—one redheaded, the other bald— holding their expanded umbrellas aloft in their left hands. I scowled in turn as both men reached up with their right hands to dust imaginary sprinkles off their left shoulders.

"No problem here," I said. "We're leaving."

"You are," the bald one said. "He's working."

"He's quitting."

"Maybe you don't hear so good." The bald one stepped closer as the redhead glanced around, no doubt checking to see if anyone was paying too much attention. "How about we go for a walk and talk where it's a little quieter?"

Though he was about six inches taller, I stared him

down. "How about you stand there and we see how clean *your* ears are."

The bald one snarled as he folded up his umbrella and started toward me. I stood my ground, raised my voice.

"You're being ripped off."

His brow furrowed as he stopped, evidently confused.

"That is, I've seen some pretty convincing evidence that your fine, respectable organization is being scammed."

"The hell are you talking about?" the redhead asked.

"Another organization with whom you do business has probably been siphoning funds from some of your accounts. Small enough for you all not to notice, until one day you do. By then you'll all be reduced to wearing overalls, if not barrels."

"Smart ass." Redhead approached. "How do you think you know this?"

I shook my head and smiled. "Not another word from me on that, until I have word from your higher ups that John Mark here can go clean and free from your organization, and that you'll all leave his mother and her business alone."

"His mother?"

I smirked. "If you can play dumb, so can I."

I circled around them, gesturing with a nod for John Mark to follow me. He hesitated, casting nervous looks at the two goons, but he soon followed. They stood their ground, talking to each other in hushed tones.

"Hey!" The redheaded one called after us. "How do we get in touch with you?"

"Get in touch with Sergeant Roxana Spiegel of the SPD. Ask her if she has any worthless colleagues that overindulge on rum cake."

———

I wasn't sure how well I could trust the Chark family to leave John Mark and his mom alone. But he was a bright kid, skillful. And with his knowledge, it wasn't hard to convince the PD that he'd be an asset. They promised to find a suitable position for him in the new year. That might help.

As for his mother—well, the city had other flower shops the syndicate could invest in, assuming they had their money right by then.

My estimation of SimSan and its business practices turned out to be more than accurate—*thank goodness.*

Once some of the senior Chark family members had found out who I was and cordially invited me to a "casual discussion," I hyped up the matter. "They think you're all a bunch of suckers," was pretty much the way I'd presented things. Fortunately, with the assistance of some old friends who were still active hackers and reasonably ethical, I managed to produce enough materials to open the family's eyes and make them seriously consider conducting an audit—however they wanted to handle *that*.

The Chark generally paid far more detailed attention to the finances of their illicit activities, trusting their more or less legit businesses to run more or less like clockwork. So long as they sensed nothing amiss, they figured nothing was amiss. But at the end of the day, money was money—and once they got the slightest sense or hint that they were being had, well then . . .

SimSan's own private, long-going, rip-off party just might get crashed. I wondered what authorities might come to their rescue.

To the Chark family, I helpfully offered Derrick Trainor's name and contact information. He could— willingly, I'm sure—assist them in looking into matters and sorting everything out. I suggested they reach out to him in person; that way they could be certain he'd go out of his way to burnish his employer's reputation in their eyes.

My reputation as a neighbor needed some polishing as well. I invited Ria and John Mark to my house for a special Christmas Eve dinner, one I spent days planning. Something I hadn't really even considered since Anuba had left.

Lemon-rosemary roasted turkey with sides of butternut squash, mini potatoes with chive butter, lemon-maple roasted carrots, and green beans with garlic, rosemary, and orange zest. For dessert: roasted maple pears with cranberries and thyme. No damned fruitcakes in sight.

Complex menu? Oh yeah—but I wasn't about to take chances with catering in this city. *I* did all the sweating in the kitchen.

Dinner was a delight, genuinely enjoyed by my guests—who I figured were neither great actors nor liars. And yet the food paled in comparison to the passionate conversations, all the tears of sadness and eventually joy, not to mention—late into the cold night—all the warm talk about a new family.

FURTHER READING

The *CRACKED SINK* Series

Welcome to The Sink

ABOUT THE AUTHOR

Harambee K. Grey-Sun is the author of several novels, novellas, and short stories, including *Hero Zero*, *Colder Than Ice*, and the story collection *Blind Dates*. For more information about his books and ongoing projects, please visit www.harambeegreysun.com.

ALSO BY HARAMBEE K. GREY-SUN

Standalone Stories

Colder Than Ice

The *GRACE OTHERWISE* Series

Blind Dates

The *HERO ZERO* Series

Hero Zero

The *EVE OF LIGHT* Series

The Lark

ArtWork

Lilith's Arithmetic: The Revelations of Artemisia Wright

BloodLight: The Apocalypse of Robert Goldner

Heaven's Gun

White Fire

Rogue Beauty

Deviant-Hunter: Blood Oath

Deviant-Hunter, Killer of Saints

Deviant-Hunter's Sabbath

Broken Angels (Eve of Light, Book I)

FoolKillers

Knotty & Ice

Divinities, Entangled (Eve of Light, Book II)

Influx

BY HARAMBEE GREY-SUN

Poetry

Spring's Fall (Autumn Numbers * Book I)

Wine Songs, Vinegar Verses

Trinity & Its Twin

www.ingramcontent.com/pod-product-compliance
Lightning Source LLC
Chambersburg PA
CBHW051928220626
47052CB00003B/626